HOW TO MAKE MILLIONS WITH AI

SAM RAMSEY

Made with ♥ on the Notion Press Platform
www.notionpress.com

Contents

Introduction v

1. Understanding Ai 1

Definition Of AI And Its Evolution

Types Of AI

Applications Of AI In Business

2. Chapter 2 9

Cost-saving Benefits Of AI

Increased Productivity With AI

Enhanced Customer Experience With AI

AI And Data-driven Decision-making

3. Identifying Opportunities For Ai 19

Defining Your AI Strategy

4. Building An Ai Team 25

Training And Managing Your AI Team

5. Chapter 5 29

AI Tools

Integrating AI Into Your Business Processes Testing And Validating Your AI Solutions

6. Scaling Your Ai Business 35

Raising Capital For Your AI Business Marketing And Selling Your AI Solutions

7. Risks And Challenges Of Ai 39

Ethical And Legal Considerations Of AI

Mitigating Risks Associated With AI Future Challenges

Contents

And Opportunities Of AI

Bonus 45

Introduction

In this book, we will explore the world of AI and how it can be used to create wealth. We will take a comprehensive look at how AI is changing the business landscape and the opportunities it presents for entrepreneurs and business leaders. By the end of this book, you will have a clear understanding of how to leverage AI to generate millions.

CHAPTER I

Understanding AI

Artificial Intelligence (AI) is a branch of computer science that aims to create intelligent machines that can perform tasks that typically require human intelligence, such as perception, reasoning, learning, and problem-solving. AI has been defined in many ways, but one common definition is "the ability of machines to perform tasks that would normally require human intelligence."

Definition of AI and its evolution

The evolution of AI can be traced back to the 1940s and 1950s, with the development of early computers and the emergence of cybernetics, the study of communication and control in animals and machines. The first AI programs were developed in the 1950s, with the goal of simulating human intelligence. The 1956 Dartmouth Conference is considered to be the birthplace of AI, as it brought together researchers who shared a common interest in the topic.

In the 1960s and 1970s, AI research was focused on rule-based systems and knowledge representation, which aimed to create systems that could reason and solve problems using a set of logical rules. However, progress was slow due to the limitations of the computing hardware and lack of data.

In the 1980s and 1990s, the focus of AI research shifted towards machine learning, which aimed to create systems that could learn from data and improve their performance over time. This led to the development of neural networks and other machine learning algorithms, which have been used in a wide range of applications, including speech recognition, image recognition, and natural language processing.

In recent years, AI has seen a resurgence in interest, driven by advances in computing power and the availability of large amounts of data. AI has been used in many applications, including autonomous vehicles, recommendation systems, and personalized medicine. The future of AI is expected to bring many exciting opportunities and challenges, as researchers work towards developing more advanced and intelligent systems.

Types of AI

1. Reactive Machines: These are the most basic types of AI systems that do not have the ability to learn from past experiences. They can only respond to the current situation based on the programmed rules. Examples include chess-playing computers and robots that perform repetitive tasks.
2. Limited Memory: These AI systems can learn from past experiences and make decisions based on that learning. They use historical data to make predictions about future events. Examples include self-driving cars and recommendation systems.
3. Theory of Mind: This is a type of AI that can understand human emotions, beliefs, and thoughts, and can use that understanding to interact with humans in a more natural way. Theory of mind is still a developing field, but it has potential applications in areas such as customer service and mental health.
4. Self-Aware: This is a hypothetical type of AI that is not yet possible. Self-aware AI would be able to understand its own existence and have a sense of consciousness.

Applications of AI in business

1. Automation: AI can automate repetitive and time-consuming tasks, such as data entry and document processing. This can free up human resources to work on more complex tasks.
2. Customer Service: AI-powered chatbots can handle customer inquiries and provide 24/7 support, improving customer satisfaction and reducing response times.
3. Marketing: AI can analyze customer data and behavior to personalize marketing campaigns and improve customer engagement.
4. Decision-Making: AI can analyze large amounts of data and provide insights that can help businesses make better decisions.
5. Supply Chain Management: AI can optimize supply chain operations by predicting demand, reducing waste, and improving delivery times.
6. Cybersecurity: AI can detect and prevent cyber threats in real-time, reducing the risk of data breaches and other security incidents.

AI has a wide range of applications in business, and its potential is still being explored. As AI technology continues to evolve, businesses are finding new and innovative ways to use it to improve their operations and gain a competitive advantage.

CHAPTER II

The business case for AI is based on the potential benefits that AI can bring to a wide range of business operations. Here are some of the key benefits:

1. Increased Efficiency: AI can automate repetitive and time-consuming tasks, freeing up employees to focus on more complex and strategic work. This can result in increased productivity, reduced labor costs, and faster response times.
2. Improved Accuracy: AI can perform tasks with high accuracy, reducing errors and the need for manual intervention. For example, AI-powered software can detect fraud and anomalies in financial transactions, reducing the need for manual audits.
3. Predictive Analytics: AI can use machine learning algorithms to analyze large amounts of data and make predictions about future events. This can help businesses make better decisions and improve their operations, such as predicting customer demand and optimizing inventory management.
4. Enhanced Customer Experience: AI can be used to provide personalized and interactive customer experiences, such as chatbots and recommendation systems. This can improve customer satisfaction and retention.
5. Cost Savings: AI can reduce costs by optimizing business processes, reducing waste, and improving energy efficiency.

6. Competitive Advantage: AI can provide businesses with a competitive advantage by enabling them to innovate and adapt to changing market conditions more quickly and effectively.

There are also some challenges and risks associated with AI, such as data privacy and security concerns, ethical considerations, and the potential for job displacement. Therefore, it is important for businesses to carefully evaluate the potential benefits and risks of AI and develop a strategy that balances these factors. AI has the potential to transform businesses and industries in significant ways, and those who are able to effectively leverage its capabilities are likely to gain a significant advantage in the marketplace.

Cost-saving benefits of AI

AI can provide a number of cost-saving benefits for businesses, including:

1. Automation of repetitive tasks: AI can automate tasks that are repetitive, time-consuming, and require little or no decision-making. This can help businesses save on labor costs and improve efficiency. For example, AI can be used to automate data entry and document processing, reducing the need for human input.
2. Improved accuracy and efficiency: AI can perform tasks with high accuracy and efficiency, reducing errors and the need for manual intervention. This can help businesses save on costs related to errors, such as rework or fines. For example, AI-powered software can detect fraud and anomalies in financial transactions, reducing the need for manual audits.
3. Predictive maintenance: AI can predict equipment failures and maintenance needs, enabling businesses to proactively address potential issues and reduce downtime. This can help businesses save on maintenance costs and improve productivity.
4. Energy efficiency: AI can optimize energy usage by adjusting settings and controlling equipment based on real-time data. This can help businesses save on energy costs and reduce their carbon footprint.
5. Optimization of supply chain operations: AI can optimize supply chain operations by predicting demand, reducing waste, and improving delivery

times. This can help businesses save on costs related to excess inventory, stockouts, and shipping delays.

6. Reduction of customer churn: AI can analyze customer data and behavior to predict which customers are at risk of leaving and provide targeted interventions to retain them. This can help businesses save on costs related to customer acquisition and improve revenue growth.

The cost-saving benefits of AI are significant, and businesses that are able to leverage its capabilities are likely to achieve a competitive advantage in the marketplace. It is important to carefully evaluate the potential benefits and costs of AI and develop a strategy that balances these factors.

Increased productivity with AI

AI can significantly increase productivity by automating tasks and enabling employees to focus on more complex and strategic work. Here are some ways in which AI can increase productivity in business:

1. Improved decision-making: AI can analyze large amounts of data and provide insights that can help businesses make better decisions. This can help to improve productivity by reducing the time and effort required to analyze data, and by providing more accurate and relevant information to decision-makers.
2. Predictive analytics: AI can use machine learning algorithms to analyze data and make predictions about future events. This can help businesses make better decisions about resource allocation, staffing, and inventory management, which can improve productivity by ensuring that resources are used more efficiently.
3. Enhanced collaboration: AI-powered collaboration tools can help employees to work together more efficiently and effectively. For example, chatbots can be used to provide real-time support and facilitate communication between team members, which can improve productivity by reducing the time and effort required to collaborate.

4. Improved customer service: AI-powered chatbots and other customer service tools can help businesses to provide faster and more personalized service to customers. This can help to improve productivity by reducing the time and effort required to respond to customer inquiries and complaints.
5. Streamlined workflows: AI can help to streamline workflows by automating tasks and identifying areas for improvement. This can help to reduce the time and effort required to complete tasks, and improve overall productivity.

AI has the potential to significantly increase productivity in business by automating routine tasks, improving decision-making, enabling collaboration, and streamlining workflows.It is important to carefully evaluate the potential benefits and costs of AI and develop a strategy that balances these factors.

Enhanced customer experience with AI

AI has the potential to significantly enhance the customer experience by providing faster, more personalized service and enabling businesses to better understand and anticipate customer needs. Here are some ways in which AI can enhance the customer experience in business:

1. Personalization: AI can help businesses to personalize the customer experience by analyzing data and providing tailored recommendations and offers. For example, AI-powered chatbots can provide personalized product recommendations and offer discounts based on a customer's purchase history.
2. Predictive analytics: AI can use machine learning algorithms to analyze data and make predictions about customer behavior. This can help businesses to better understand and anticipate customer needs, and provide more personalized service. For example, AI can analyze a customer's purchase history and predict what products they are likely to buy in the future.
3. Chatbots and virtual assistants: AI-powered chatbots and virtual assistants can provide real-time support to customers, helping them to quickly and easily find the information they need. This can help to reduce the time and effort required to provide customer service, and improve overall customer satisfaction.

4. Voice assistants: Voice assistants like Amazon Alexa and Google Assistant can be used to provide personalized service to customers in their homes or workplaces. For example, a customer could use a voice assistant to order groceries, book a restaurant reservation, or find out about local events.
5. 24/7 availability: AI-powered chatbots and virtual assistants can be available 24/7, providing customers with immediate support and reducing the need for human intervention. This can help to improve the customer experience by reducing wait times and improving overall responsiveness.
6. Sentiment analysis: AI can analyze customer feedback and sentiment to identify areas for improvement and address customer concerns. This can help businesses to better understand their customers and improve the customer experience.

AI has the potential to significantly enhance the customer experience by providing personalized service, anticipating customer needs, and improving responsiveness. It is important to carefully evaluate the potential benefits and costs of AI and develop a strategy that balances these factors.

AI and data-driven decision-making

AI and data-driven decision-making go hand in hand. AI can process and analyze vast amounts of data quickly and accurately, providing valuable insights that can help businesses make better decisions. Here are some ways in which AI can enhance data-driven decision-making in business:

1. Data analysis: AI can analyze large amounts of data and identify patterns and trends that may not be immediately apparent to humans. This can help businesses to make more informed decisions based on data-driven insights.
2. Predictive analytics: AI can use machine learning algorithms to analyze data and make predictions about future events. This can help businesses to anticipate and prepare for future trends and opportunities, and make proactive decisions based on data-driven insights.
3. Real-time data analysis: AI can analyze data in real-time, providing businesses with up-to-the-minute insights that can help them make more informed decisions. For example, AI can analyze customer data in real-time to provide businesses with insights into customer behavior and preferences.
4. Risk analysis: AI can be used to analyze data and identify potential risks and opportunities. This can

help businesses to make more informed decisions and mitigate risks before they become problematic.

5. Improved accuracy: AI can analyze data with greater accuracy and consistency than humans, reducing the likelihood of errors and providing more reliable insights.

AI can significantly enhance data-driven decision-making by providing businesses with insights and predictions based on vast amounts of data. It is important to carefully evaluate the potential benefits and costs of AI and develop a strategy that balances these factors. Additionally, it is important to ensure that data is of high quality and appropriate for analysis to ensure the accuracy and reliability of AI-driven insights.

CHAPTER III

Identifying Opportunities for AI

Assessing your business needs is a crucial step in identifying opportunities for AI. It involves understanding your business goals and objectives, as well as your operational and technological requirements. Here are some steps you can take to assess your business needs:

Define your business goals: Identify your short-term and long-term business goals, and the key performance indicators (KPIs) that are critical to achieving those goals. This will help you to identify areas where AI can help you achieve those goals more effectively.

- Analyze your business processes: Analyze your existing business processes to identify areas where AI can improve efficiency, productivity, and cost-effectiveness. For example, identify repetitive or time-consuming tasks that can be automated with AI, or areas where AI can help to improve decision-making processes.
- Understand your data requirements: Identify the types of data that your business needs to operate effectively, as well as the quality and quantity of data that is required. This will help you to identify areas where AI can help you to collect, process, and analyze data more effectively.
- Assess your technology infrastructure: Evaluate your existing technology infrastructure to identify areas where AI can be integrated into your existing systems and processes. This will help you to identify areas where AI can help to improve efficiency and effectiveness, and

to identify potential integration challenges.

- Identify areas for innovation: Identify areas where your business can benefit from innovative applications of AI, or where new AI-based products or services can be developed to meet evolving customer needs.

Assessing your business needs involves a systematic analysis of your business goals, processes, data requirements, technology infrastructure, and areas for innovation. This will help you to identify opportunities for AI that align with your business needs and can provide competitive advantage.

Identifying areas where AI can be integrated into your business is a key step in identifying opportunities for AI. Here are some steps you can take to identify areas for integration:

- Evaluate your existing systems and processes: Assess your existing systems and processes to identify areas where AI can be integrated. For example, look for areas where data is collected, analyzed, or used for decision-making.
- Identify opportunities for automation: Look for areas where AI can be used to automate repetitive or time-consuming tasks. For example, AI can be used to automate data entry, data processing, or customer service tasks.
- Look for areas where AI can improve decision-making: Look for areas where AI can be used to improve decision-making processes. For example, AI can be used to analyze data and provide insights that can help to inform business decisions.

- Identify areas where AI can enhance the customer experience: Look for areas where AI can be used to enhance the customer experience. For example, AI can be used to provide personalized recommendations, to enable customers to interact with your business through chatbots or virtual assistants, or to provide real-time support.
- Assess the feasibility of integration: Evaluate the technical feasibility of integrating AI into your existing systems and processes. Consider factors such as the availability of data, the need for additional infrastructure or resources, and the potential impact on existing processes.

Identifying areas where AI can be integrated involves a systematic analysis of your existing systems and processes, as well as your business goals and objectives. It is important to carefully evaluate potential areas for integration and develop a strategy that balances the potential benefits and costs of AI, as well as ensuring that data is of high quality and appropriate for analysis.

Defining your AI strategy

Defining your AI strategy involves identifying the specific areas where AI can provide the most value to your business, and developing a plan to implement AI in those areas. To define your AI strategy, you should start by identifying your business goals and objectives, and then assess how AI can help you achieve those goals. This involves evaluating your existing systems and processes, as well as your data infrastructure and technology capabilities, to identify areas where AI can improve efficiency, productivity, or cost-effectiveness.

Once you have identified the areas where AI can be most effective, you can develop a plan to implement AI in those areas. This plan should include a roadmap for integrating AI into your existing systems and processes, as well as a plan for developing and acquiring the necessary technology and data resources. It is also important to consider the potential impact on your workforce, and develop a plan for upskilling or reskilling employees to work with AI.

Ultimately, your AI strategy should be aligned with your overall business strategy and goals, and should be designed to provide competitive advantage by leveraging the power of AI to improve efficiency, productivity, and innovation.

CHAPTER IV

Building an AI Team

Building an AI team requires identifying the right talent to develop and implement AI solutions that align with your business goals. Here are some steps you can take to recruit the right talent for your AI team:

Define your job roles and responsibilities: Define the job roles and responsibilities for your AI team, including data scientists, machine learning engineers, and software developers. You should also consider hiring a project manager to oversee your AI initiatives.

Identify the skills and experience you need: Identify the skills and experience you need for each job role. This may include skills such as programming languages (Python, R, Java), machine learning frameworks (TensorFlow, Keras, PyTorch), and data analysis and visualization tools.

Develop a job description and post job openings: Develop a job description that clearly outlines the job responsibilities, required skills and experience, and qualifications. Post the job openings on job boards, social media, and industry-specific websites to reach potential candidates.

Assess candidates for cultural fit: Assess candidates for cultural fit by looking at their work experience, skills, and personality. You should also consider the candidate's communication skills, ability to work in a team, and willingness to learn new skills.

Provide ongoing training and development: Provide ongoing training and development opportunities for your AI team to help them stay up to date with the latest AI trends and technologies. You can provide in-house training, send employees to conferences and workshops, or provide access to online learning resources.

Recruiting the right talent is crucial to building an effective AI team that can drive innovation and growth in your business. By following these steps, you can identify and attract top talent that can help you achieve your AI goals and objectives.

Training and Managing your AI team

Managing your AI team requires ongoing training and development to ensure that your team is up-to-date with the latest AI technologies and methodologies. Here are some steps you can take to train and manage your AI team effectively:

- Provide training and development opportunities: Provide ongoing training and development opportunities for your AI team to help them stay current with the latest AI trends and technologies. This can include in-house training, sending employees to conferences and workshops, or providing access to online learning resources.
- Encourage collaboration and communication: Encourage collaboration and communication among your AI team members to promote knowledge sharing and idea generation. This can include regular team meetings, brainstorming sessions, and cross-functional projects.
- Set clear goals and objectives: Set clear goals and objectives for your AI team to help focus their efforts and measure their progress. This can include both short-term and long-term goals, such as improving accuracy rates, reducing processing times, or developing new AI applications.

- Provide feedback and recognition: Provide feedback and recognition to your AI team members to help them understand their strengths and areas for improvement. This can include regular performance reviews, coaching and mentoring, and recognition for achievements.
- Manage resources effectively: Manage your resources effectively to ensure that your AI team has the necessary tools and infrastructure to support their work. This can include investing in hardware and software, collaborating with IT and other departments to address technical issues, and prioritizing projects based on their strategic value.
- Monitor and evaluate team performance: Monitor and evaluate your AI team's performance regularly to ensure that they are meeting their goals and objectives. This can include tracking key performance indicators such as accuracy rates, productivity, and ROI, and making adjustments as needed to optimize team performance.

By following these steps, you can train and manage your AI team effectively to ensure that they are delivering value to your business. A well-trained and motivated AI team can help you achieve your business goals and stay competitive in your industry.

CHAPTER V

Implementing AI in your business requires identifying the right AI tools and technologies that can help you achieve your business goals. Here are some steps you can take to identify the right AI tools and technologies for your business:

Identify your AI use cases: Identify the specific use cases for AI in your business. This may include areas such as customer service, marketing, finance, or operations.

Evaluate available AI tools and technologies: Evaluate the available AI tools and technologies that can help you address your use cases. This may include natural language processing (NLP) tools, machine learning algorithms, predictive analytics models, and chatbots.

Assess the usability and compatibility of AI tools: Assess the usability and compatibility of the AI tools and technologies you are considering. This may include evaluating the ease of use, scalability, and integration with your existing systems.

Consider the vendor's reputation and support: Consider the vendor's reputation and level of support when selecting AI tools and technologies. Look for vendors with a proven track record of success and responsive support services.

Develop a plan for testing and deployment: Develop a plan for testing and deploying the AI tools and technologies. This should include identifying the data sources needed for training the AI models, developing testing protocols, and implementing the AI solution in a phased approach.

AI tools

There are numerous AI tools and technologies available in the market, and choosing the right ones can be overwhelming. Here are some examples of popular AI tools and websites:

1. TensorFlow: TensorFlow is an open-source machine learning library that is used to build and train deep learning models.
2. Keras: Keras is a high-level neural networks API, written in Python and capable of running on top of TensorFlow, that simplifies the process of building deep learning models.
3. PyTorch: PyTorch is an open-source machine learning framework that is used to develop deep learning models.
4. IBM Watson: IBM Watson is a cloud-based AI platform that offers a range of AI services, such as language understanding, speech-to-text, and visual recognition.
5. Google Cloud AI: Google Cloud AI is a suite of machine learning and AI tools that allow businesses to build and deploy AI models at scale.
6. Amazon AI: Amazon AI is a set of services and tools that allow businesses to build and deploy intelligent applications quickly and easily.
7. DataRobot: DataRobot is an AI platform that automates the end-to-end process of building and deploying AI models, from data preparation to model deployment.

8. Hugging Face: Hugging Face is an open-source platform that provides pre-trained models and tools for natural language processing (NLP) tasks, such as language translation and sentiment analysis.

When choosing an AI tool or technology, it is important to consider your business needs, technical expertise, and budget. It is also important to evaluate the features and capabilities of each tool to ensure that it meets your specific requirements.

Integrating AI into your business processes Testing and validating your AI solutions

Integrating AI into your business processes can be a complex process, but testing and validating your AI solutions can help ensure that they meet your business needs and deliver accurate results. Here are some best practices for testing and validating AI solutions:

- Data preparation: Before testing your AI solutions, it is important to prepare the data that will be used for testing. This involves collecting relevant data, cleaning it, and organizing it in a way that is compatible with your AI algorithms.
- Test data selection: It is important to select the right test data to validate your AI solutions. This means ensuring that your test data is representative of the real-world data your AI solutions will be processing, but is different enough to avoid overfitting.
- Evaluation metrics: It is important to establish evaluation metrics that measure the accuracy and effectiveness of your AI solutions. These metrics should be aligned with your business goals and objectives, and should be used to guide the

development and optimization of your AI models.

- Validation techniques: There are various validation techniques that can be used to test and validate AI solutions, such as cross-validation, holdout validation, and leave-one-out validation. These techniques help to assess the performance of your AI models and ensure that they are working as expected.
- Iterative testing: Testing and validating your AI solutions should be an iterative process, where you continually refine your models and algorithms based on feedback from your validation results. This allows you to identify and fix any issues or errors before deploying your AI solutions in a live environment.

By following these best practices, you can ensure that your AI solutions are robust and reliable, and are capable of delivering accurate results that support your business objectives. It is important to remember that AI solutions are not a one-time implementation, and require continuous monitoring and optimization to ensure that they remain effective and relevant.

CHAPTER VI

Scaling Your AI Business

Scaling your AI business requires developing a sustainable business model that allows you to leverage the capabilities of AI to create innovative products and services that meet the needs of your customers. One way to do this is by using AI tools and platforms such as OpenAI and Chat GPT to create books, stories, and other content that can be sold or licensed to customers.

For example, you could develop a product that uses AI to generate unique and engaging stories or articles, which can be sold to publishers or online media outlets. You could also use AI to develop chatbots or virtual assistants that can help customers with their inquiries, providing a more personalized and efficient customer experience.

Another approach is to leverage AI to improve your internal business processes, such as automating repetitive tasks or improving your supply chain management. This can help you streamline your operations, reduce costs, and improve your overall efficiency, which can translate into a competitive advantage and increased profitability.

To develop a sustainable business model for your AI business, it is important to understand the unique capabilities and limitations of AI, as well as the needs and preferences of your customers. You should also invest in the right talent and technology to support your AI initiatives, and be willing to iterate and experiment to find the right approach for your business. By taking a strategic and customer-centric approach to your AI initiatives, you can create a sustainable and profitable business that leverages the power of AI to deliver value to your customers.

Raising capital for your AI business Marketing and selling your AI solutions

Once you have developed your AI solutions and established a sustainable business model, you may need to raise capital to fund your growth and expansion. There are several ways to do this, including venture capital funding, private equity, crowdfunding, or strategic partnerships with other companies in your industry.

To attract investors or partners, you will need to demonstrate the value and potential of your AI solutions, as well as your ability to execute on your business plan. This may involve developing a compelling pitch deck or business plan that highlights the unique features and benefits of your products or services, as well as your target market and competitive positioning.

You will also need to focus on marketing and selling your AI solutions to your target customers. This may involve developing targeted marketing campaigns that leverage the unique features and benefits of your AI products, as well as engaging in content marketing or thought leadership to build your brand and reputation in the industry.

Ultimately, the key to successfully marketing and selling your AI solutions is to focus on delivering real value to your customers. By developing products that meet their needs and solve their problems, you can build a loyal customer base and create a sustainable and profitable business that leverages the power of AI to drive growth and innovation.

CHAPTER VII

Risks and Challenges of AI

While AI has the potential to bring significant benefits to businesses and society, it also poses a number of risks and challenges that must be addressed. One of the biggest risks of AI is the potential for biased or unfair decision-making, particularly when AI algorithms are trained on biased data or models.

Other risks of AI include the potential for cyber attacks or other security breaches that could compromise sensitive data, as well as the potential for job displacement or economic disruption as AI and automation continue to replace human workers in certain industries. Additionally, there are concerns about the ethical implications of using AI in fields such as healthcare, where decisions made by AI algorithms could have significant and potentially life-altering consequences for patients.

To address these risks and challenges, it is important to take a responsible and ethical approach to AI development and implementation. This may involve developing clear guidelines and best practices for the ethical use of AI, as well as investing in ongoing research and development to ensure that AI systems are transparent, accountable, and equitable.

It is also important to engage in ongoing dialogue with stakeholders, including employees, customers, and industry experts, to understand the potential risks and impacts of AI on their lives and livelihoods, and to develop strategies for mitigating these risks and ensuring that the benefits of AI are shared more widely.

Ultimately, the success of AI will depend on our ability to address these risks and challenges in a responsible and proactive manner, while also leveraging the full potential of AI to drive innovation, growth, and positive change in our businesses and society as a whole.

Ethical and legal considerations of AI

As AI becomes increasingly pervasive in our businesses and society, it is important to consider the ethical and legal implications of this technology. Ethical considerations include the potential for biased or discriminatory decision-making, as well as concerns around privacy and data protection. In addition, there is a growing concern around the accountability and transparency of AI algorithms and how decisions made by these systems can be audited or challenged.

From a legal perspective, there are a number of potential issues related to AI, including intellectual property rights, liability and responsibility for decisions made by AI systems, and compliance with regulations and standards. For example, there may be questions around who owns the intellectual property rights to an AI system, or who is responsible when an AI system makes a decision that causes harm or violates a regulation.

To address these ethical and legal considerations, it is important for businesses to develop clear guidelines and best practices for the ethical and responsible use of AI. This may involve engaging with stakeholders to understand their concerns and perspectives, as well as investing in ongoing research and development to ensure that AI systems are transparent, accountable, and equitable.

In addition, it is important to ensure that AI systems are compliant with relevant regulations and standards, and to work closely with legal and regulatory experts to navigate any potential legal challenges or risks associated with AI implementation.

Ultimately, the responsible and ethical use of AI will require ongoing attention and investment, both in terms of developing new technologies and ensuring that these technologies are used in a way that aligns with our values and principles as a society. By working together to address these considerations, we can help to ensure that AI is used in a way that supports our businesses, our communities, and our shared future.

Mitigating risks associated with AI Future challenges and opportunities of AI

While AI presents many opportunities for businesses and society as a whole, it also brings with it a number of risks and challenges. Some of the key risks associated with AI include:

1. Bias and discrimination: One of the biggest risks associated with AI is the potential for bias and discrimination, particularly when it comes to decision-making. This can occur when AI algorithms are trained on biased or incomplete data, or when they are programmed with biased decision-making rules. This can result in unfair treatment of certain groups or individuals.
2. Privacy and data protection: AI systems rely on large amounts of data to make decisions, and there is a risk that this data can be compromised or misused. This can lead to privacy violations, data breaches, or other security risks.
3. Safety and security: As AI becomes increasingly integrated into our physical world, there is a risk that it could create safety and security risks. For example, autonomous vehicles or drones could malfunction and cause harm to people or property.

4. Economic disruption: As AI becomes more advanced, there is a risk that it could disrupt certain industries and lead to job loss or other economic challenges.

To mitigate these risks, it is important for businesses and policymakers to take a proactive approach to AI development and deployment. This may involve developing ethical guidelines for AI, investing in research and development to ensure that AI is transparent, accountable, and fair, and working to educate the public and policymakers about the potential risks and benefits of AI.

In addition, it is important to invest in measures to ensure the safety and security of AI systems, such as developing robust testing and validation processes, implementing security protocols to protect data, and working to ensure that AI systems are not vulnerable to cyberattacks or other security threats.

Looking to the future, there are a number of challenges and opportunities associated with AI. On the one hand, AI has the potential to drive significant innovation and economic growth, and to solve some of the world's most pressing problems. However, it also presents a number of complex ethical, legal, and social challenges that will need to be addressed. As AI continues to evolve, it will be important for businesses and society as a whole to work together to ensure that it is developed and used in a responsible and ethical way that aligns with our values and principles as a society.

Bonus

In 2023, there are many opportunities to make money with AI. Here are a few suggestions:

- Develop AI applications: Develop AI-based applications that can solve real-world problems or meet specific needs of businesses. You can use tools like TensorFlow, PyTorch, or scikit-learn to develop AI models.
- Provide AI consulting services: Many businesses want to leverage the power of AI but don't have the in-house expertise to do so. You can offer AI consulting services to help these businesses develop AI strategies and implement AI solutions.
- Build AI-powered products: You can create AI-powered products that can help people in their day-to-day lives. For example, you can develop a personal assistant app that can automate tasks, or a chatbot that can answer customer queries.
- Offer AI training: As the demand for AI skills continues to grow, you can offer training and workshops to help individuals and organizations build their AI capabilities.
- Sell data: You can build an AI-powered data analysis tool that can extract insights from data and sell this data to businesses looking to improve their operations.
- Invest in AI: With the growing interest in AI, there are many opportunities to invest in AI companies and start-ups.

Overall, making money with AI in 2023 requires creativity and a solid understanding of AI technology and its applications. Keep in mind that AI is a rapidly evolving field, and it's important to stay up-to-date with the latest developments and trends.

Printed by Libri Plureos GmbH in Hamburg,
Germany